JASPER

The Fish Who Saved a Marriage

Steven J. Simmons

illustrated by
Ray Bartkus

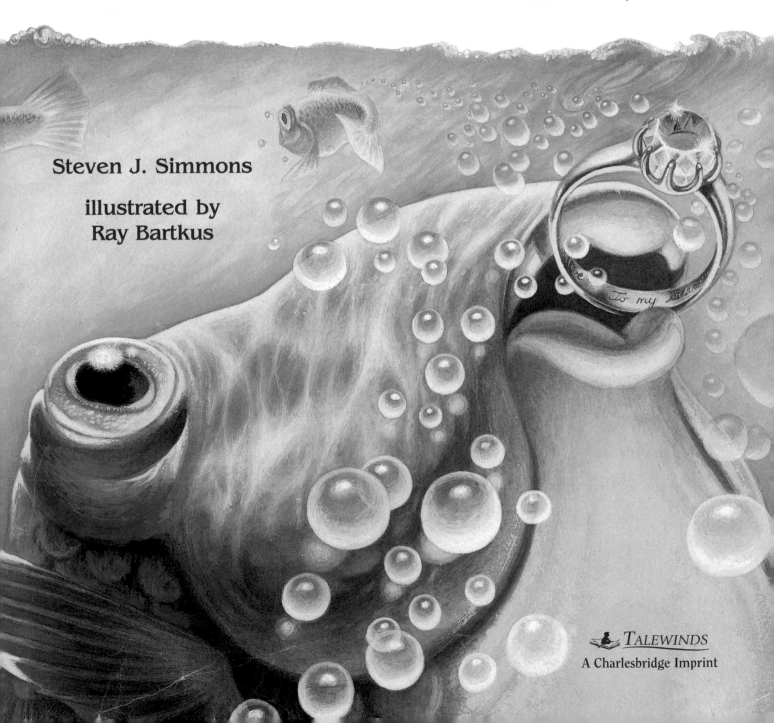

TALEWINDS

A Charlesbridge Imprint

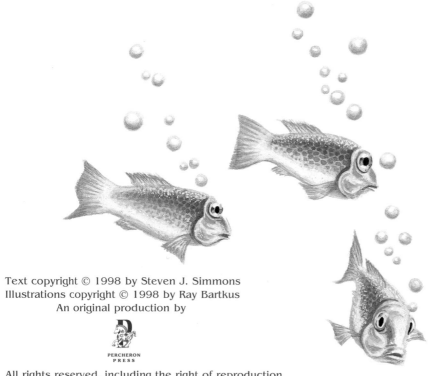

A *TALEWINDS* Book
Published by Charlesbridge Publishing
85 Main Street, Watertown, MA 02172-4411
(617) 926-0329

Library of Congress Cataloging-in-Publication Data
Simmons, Steven J., 1946–
Jasper: the fish who saved a marriage/Steven J. Simmons;
illustrated by Ray Bartkus.
p. cm.
ISBN 0-88106-989-2 (reinforced for library use)
Summary: A series of fortuitous coincidences bring together
a hungry fish, a loving couple, and a young girl.
[1. Fishes—Fiction. 2. Lost and Found possessions—Fiction.]
I. Bartkus, Ray, ill. II. Title.
P27.S59186Jas 1998
[E]—dc21 97-14271
CIP
AC

Printed in the United States of America
(hc) 10 9 8 7 6 5 4 3 2 1

The illustrations in this book were done in watercolors and acrylics on Waterford paper.
The display type and text type were set in Impact, Quake, Freeport, Clearface, and Benguiat.
Color separations were made by Eastern Rainbow Inc., Derry, New Hampshire.
Printed and bound by Worzalla Publishing Company, Stevens Point, Wisconsin
This book was printed on recycled paper.
Art direction by Sallie Baldwin
Production supervision by Brian G. Walker
Designed by Diane M. Earley

To Mom, who told the first stories, and to
Julia Stephanie, who caught the first fish.
—S.J.S.

To my son, Kris.
—R.B.

Once there was a fish called Jasper who lived off the island of Martha's Vineyard. Jasper was always hungry. He would eat everything and anything—large or small— it didn't matter. Jasper just liked to eat.

Jasper also liked to watch people on the shore of the island. One summer day as he grabbed a bite to eat, Jasper noticed a man and a woman standing at the railing of a dock. They seemed very much in love.

They were Mr. Green and his dear friend Ms. Honeycutt. At that moment, Mr. Green had a surprise for Ms. Honeycutt. He took a blue velvet box from his pocket and lifted the lid. Inside was a diamond engagement ring.

Ms. Honeycutt gently lifted the ring out of the box and read the inscription engraved inside the band:

To my beloved, I am the luckiest man alive.

"This ring was my great-grandmother's," said Mr. Green. "She always said that it brought her good luck and great joy in her marriage. It's been passed down for generations and now I'd like you to have it. Will you marry me?"

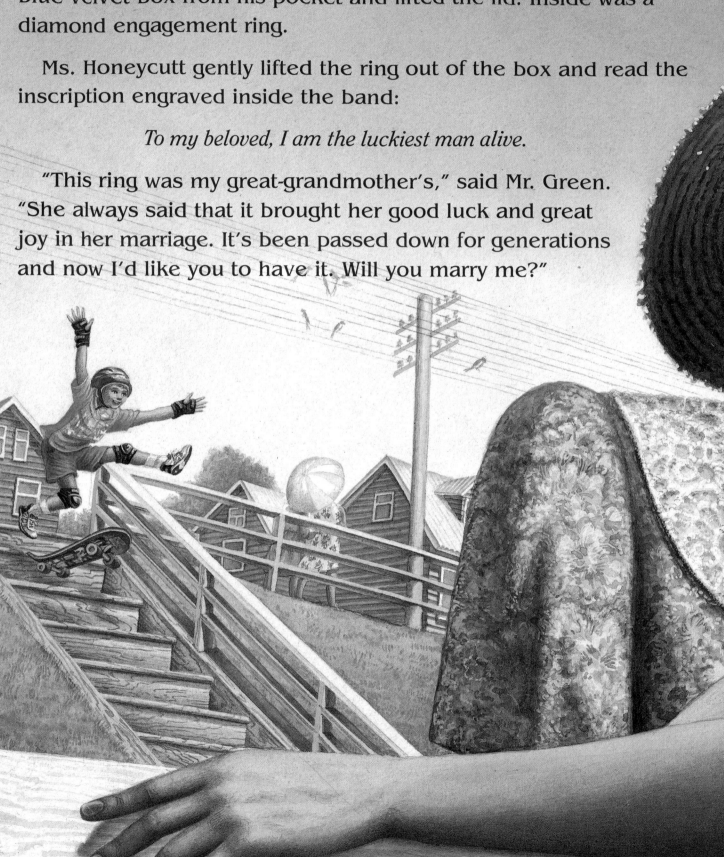

"Oh, sweetheart, of course I . . .,"
Ms. Honeycutt started to say. But
before she could finish, a boy on a
skateboard whizzed past, knocking her
against the railing. The ring went sailing
out of her hand and into the water.

Down,
   down,
      down it went.
Jasper saw the ring pass right
in front of him. It looked shiny and delicious,
so—GULP!—into his mouth it went.
      On the dock, Ms. Honeycutt burst into tears. Mr.
            Green comforted her. "Don't worry,"
                  he said. "I'll get you another ring."

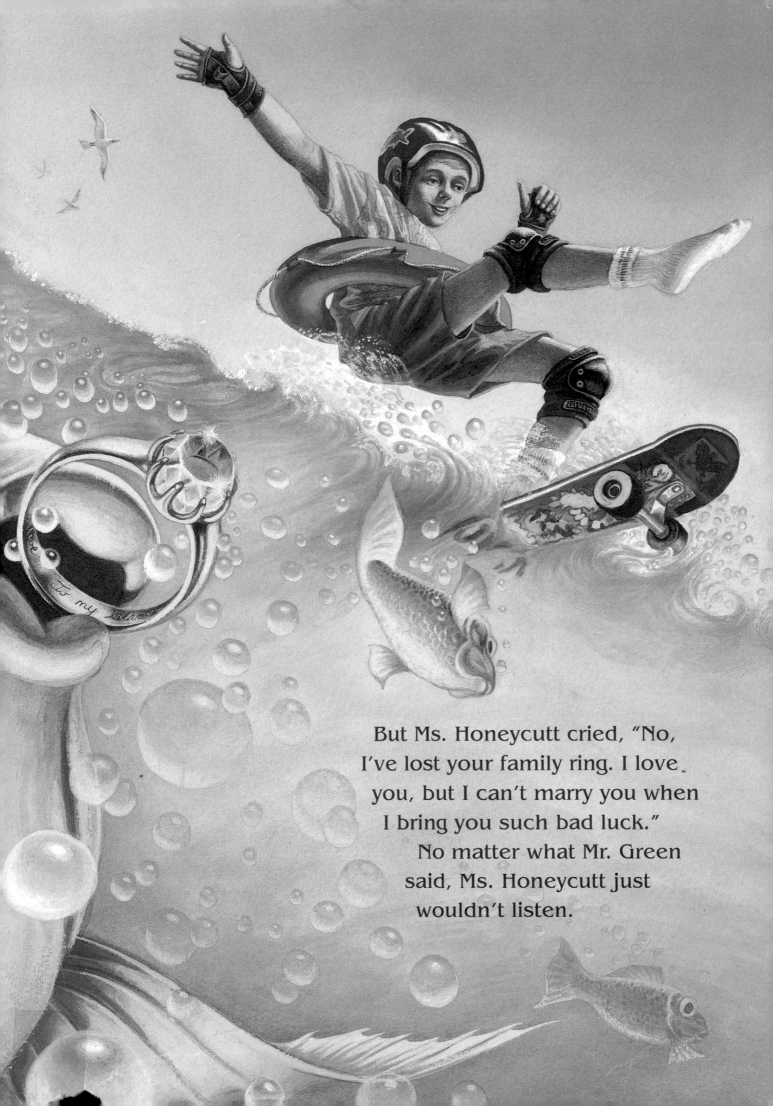

But Ms. Honeycutt cried, "No, I've lost your family ring. I love you, but I can't marry you when I bring you such bad luck." No matter what Mr. Green said, Ms. Honeycutt just wouldn't listen.

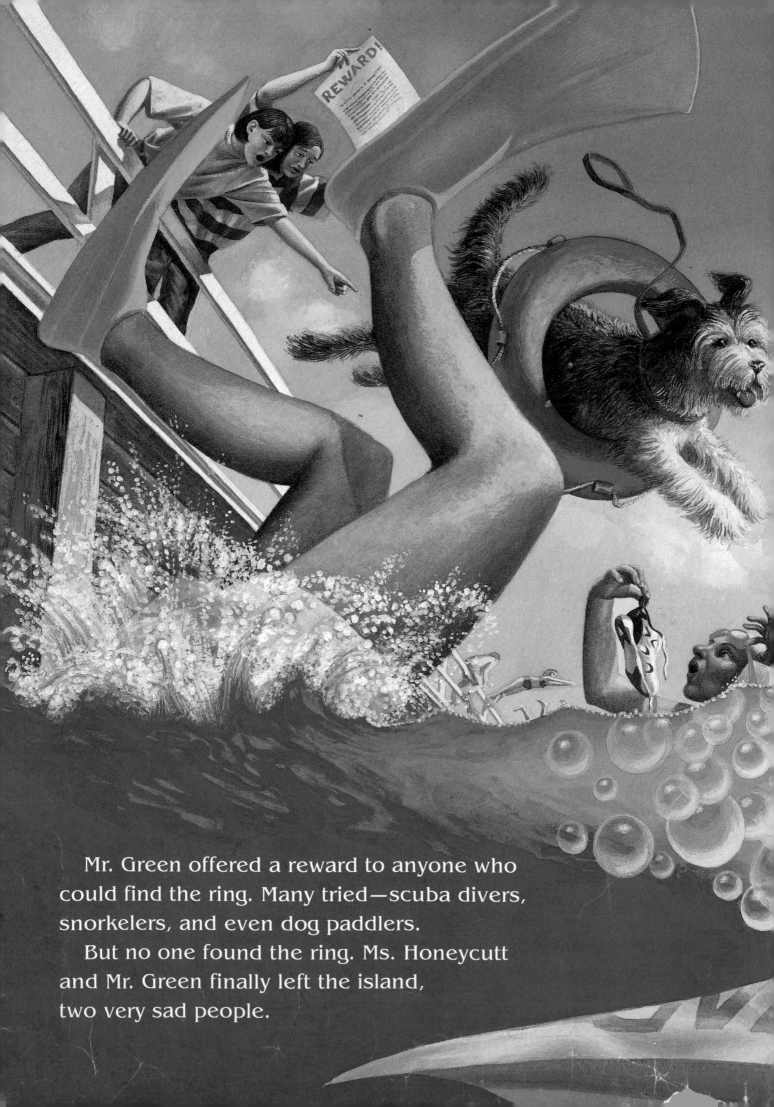

Mr. Green offered a reward to anyone who could find the ring. Many tried—scuba divers, snorkelers, and even dog paddlers.

But no one found the ring. Ms. Honeycutt and Mr. Green finally left the island, two very sad people.

A few days later, a young girl named Julia and her dad were fishing at the very same dock. Jasper was swimming below. When he saw the wriggly worm on Julia's fishhook—GULP!—down it went.

Julia felt a tug on her line and reeled it in.

"Dad, look!" Julia exclaimed. "That's the most beautiful fish I've ever seen. I want to keep him."

"Keep him?" asked her father. "You mean as a pet?"

Julia nodded. Her dad looked down at his daughter and rumpled her hair. "Oh, okay," he said with a smile. "What are you going to call him?"

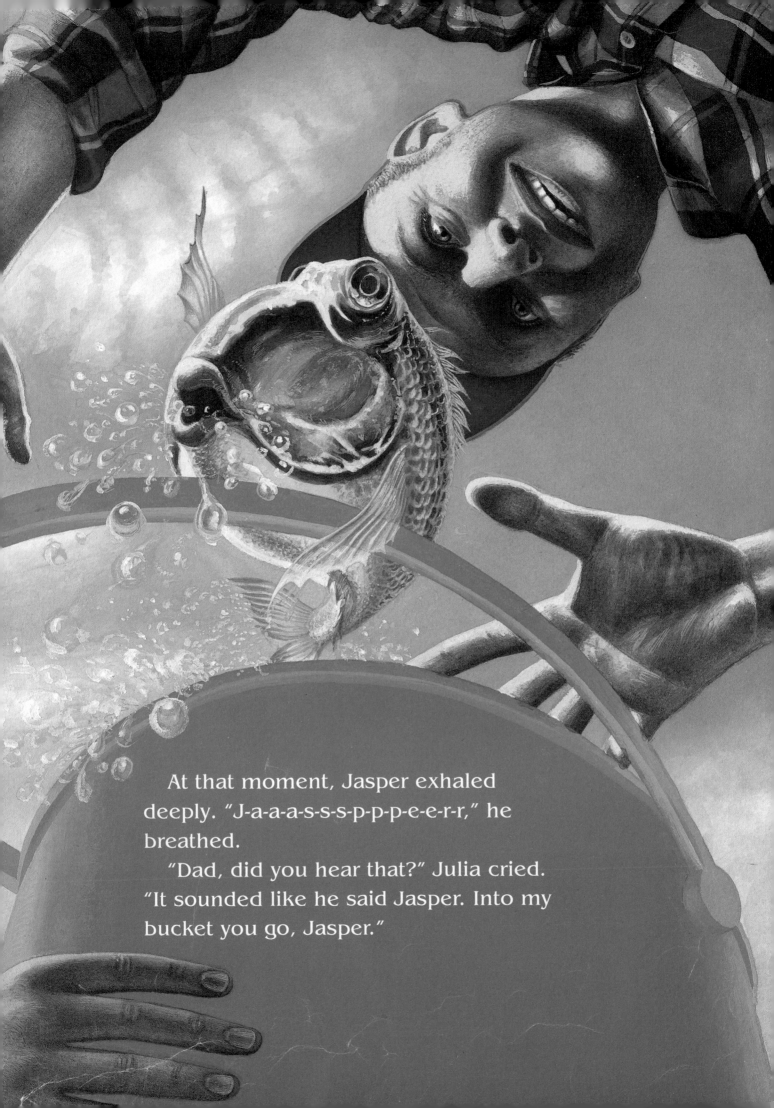

At that moment, Jasper exhaled deeply. "J-a-a-a-s-s-s-p-p-p-e-e-r-r," he breathed.

"Dad, did you hear that?" Julia cried. "It sounded like he said Jasper. Into my bucket you go, Jasper."

When Julia's family traveled home from Martha's Vineyard, they took the ferry from the island to the mainland. Julia held Jasper's bowl on the railing so that he could see the sights above the water. But Jasper only had eyes for the candy sold on board.

Back home, Julia kept Jasper in a special saltwater tank in her bedroom. She spent all her allowance at the pet store making sure he always had enough to eat.

When school started, Julia's
new teacher asked each student
to bring in one thing from summer vacation.
One child brought a tennis racket, another a mouse,
and another a butterfly collection. The teacher brought
a seashell from Martha's Vineyard, but she didn't seem
to want to talk about her trip.

Julia brought Jasper. She told the class
how she had caught Jasper and decided to
take him home.

On her way back to her desk, Julia stumbled over a friend's backpack. She managed not to fall, but Jasper's bowl tipped. Water sloshed out and Jasper sloshed out with it.

Turning somersaults as he fell, Jasper's mouth flew open in surprise. Out popped the diamond ring!

A startled Ms. Honeycutt caught Jasper
and the ring. "Goodness gracious," she
said. "This ring looks like . . . Julia, where
did you say you caught this fish?"

When Julia told her, Ms. Honeycutt took
a deep breath, turned the ring over, and
read the inscription aloud:

"To my beloved, I am the luckiest man. . . "

"Julia, you found my ring!" she gasped, sweeping Julia up in a big hug. "This is the ring I lost this summer. Oh, Julia, thank you! You and Jasper will get the reward!"

Slipping the ring safely on her finger, Ms. Honeycutt said, "Boys and girls, Principal Wathey will take over for a moment—won't you, Bill? I'll be right back." Then she squeezed past the astonished principal and ran to the school office to call Mr. Green.

Ms. Honeycutt and
Mr. Green were married
the very next week. Mr.
Green insisted that Jasper and
Julia play a very special role at
the wedding. After all, without
them, there would have been no
wedding. But he asked Jasper not to
swallow anything and Jasper didn't . . .

. . . at least not until after the ceremony.